TITCHY WITCH

AND THE FORBIDDEN FOREST

For Kitty
R.I.

For Freddie and Jake with lots of love
K.M.

ORCHARD BOOKS
338 Euston Road
London NW1 3BH
Orchard Books Australia
Level 17/207 Kent Street, Sydney, NSW 2000

First published in Great Britain in 2013
First paperback publication 2014
ISBN 978 1 40830 715 1 (HB)
ISBN 978 1 40830 719 9 (PB)
Text © Rose Impey 2013 Illustrations © Katharine McEwen 2013
A CIP catalogue record for this book is available from the British Library

1 3 5 7 9 10 8 6 4 2 (HB)
1 3 5 7 9 10 8 6 4 2 (PB)
Printed in China

Orchard Books is a division of Hachette Children's Books, an Hachette UK company.
www.hachette.co.uk

TITCHY WITCH

AND THE FORBIDDEN FOREST

BY ROSE IMPEY   ILLUSTRATED BY KATHARINE McEWEN

ORCHARD

Titchy-witch

Victor

Eric

Wendel

Weeny-witch

Witchy-witch

Cat-a-bogus

Titchy-witch was packing her case.
She was off to visit her grandma.

The bad news was Mum and Dad were too busy to go with her. Cat-a-bogus was going instead, and Titchy-witch wasn't happy about it.

"You can't fly all that way on your own," Witchy-witch told her. "What if you were to fall off your broomstick?"

Fall off! Titchy-witch was quite sure she could fly there and back, standing on her head, without falling off.

But when she spotted Grand-witch's castle, Titchy-witch got so excited she completely forgot to hold on. Luckily, Cat-a-bogus was there to catch her.

Grand-witch gave Titchy-witch a big witchy hug. "You look so like your mummy!" she told her.

"Let me show you all the lovely places that *she* liked to play when she was a little witch."

Grand-witch showed Titchy-witch
the spiral staircase that
Witchy-witch loved
to slide
down...

...and the enchanted lake she liked to jump into.

Then Grand-witch showed
Titchy-witch the attic where she
still kept all her mum's old toys.

But there was one place
Titchy-witch was *not* allowed to go
– *under any circumstances.*
And that was the Forbidden Forest.
"Far too dangerous, my little
charmer," said Grand-witch.

For a while, there was so much
to do that Titchy-witch was
perfectly
happy...

But when Grand-witch and
Cat-a-bogus started swapping spells
and recipes, Titchy-witch began to
feel a little bit bored.

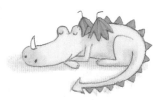

What was so *special*, anyway,
about a forbidden forest, she
wondered. It couldn't hurt
to have a closer look.
After all, no one
would know.

But Cat-a-bogus knew. He seemed
to have eyes in the end of his tail.
"I was only looking!"
Titchy-witch insisted.
"Of course you were, my little
dreamer," Grand-witch agreed.

The truth was, Titchy-witch wanted to do more than just look. And she knew exactly what she needed.

"An invisibility spell!" she told Dido.

Ghosties and spectres, fog, mist and dew,
Make me a spell that will hide us from view

In seconds Titchy-witch and Dido
started to disappear.

Titchy-witch was so excited she didn't even wait for the spell to finish working.

Straight away her little feet started running...

...through the
gate into the Forbidden Forest.
At first it felt quite exciting...

But soon the forest became *so big*...

and *so dark*...

and *sooo* creepy...

Titchy-witch's little feet raced back to the gate. But it had already closed fast behind them.

Titchy-witch didn't want to be in the Forbidden Forest at night — on her own — without any supper. She was so happy when she heard Grand-witch calling her name.

But when she tried to call back,
Titchy-witch found that her voice
had disappeared too.
Suddenly she had a very clever idea.

Titchy-witch squeezed her feet — and
the tip of Dido's tail — under the gate.
When Grand-witch spotted them,
she soon realised what had happened.

She opened the gate, then made a
quick unravelling spell.

Zig-a-zag-a-zippididoo!
Bring that precious pair into view!

First Titchy-witch and
Dido grew some legs...

then a body...

and finally a head each.
Titchy-witch was so
happy to
be back.

Later Grand-witch told Titchy-witch lots of stories about the funny things Witchy-witch got up to when she was a little witch.

Then Cat-a-bogus made his special tadpole and treacle pancakes.

So Titchy-witch was very glad to have a mouth back again — and a tummy — to put them into.

TITCHY WITCH

BY ROSE IMPEY ILLUSTRATED BY KATHARINE McEWEN

Enjoy a little more magic with all the Titchy-witch tales:

Orchard Books are available from all good
bookshops, or can be ordered from our website:
www.orchardbooks.co.uk
or telephone 01235 827702, or fax 01235 827703.

Prices and availability are subject to change.